اللهم عافني في بدني، اللهم عافني في سمعي، اللهم عافني في بصري

-Oh Allah, Grant Health to my body, Oh Allah.

- Grant health to my hearing, Oh Allah,

-Grant health to my sight

- اللهم إني أسألك الجنة وأعوذ بك من النار .

Oh Allah, I ask For Paradise, and Protection from the fire

اللهم إني أسألك برحمتك التي وسعت كل شي أن تغفر لي

O Allaah , I ask you by your mercy which envelopes all things , that you forgive me

- حسبي الله ونعم الوكيل

Allaah is sufficient for me . and how fine a trustee he is

لا حول ولا قوة إلا بالله -

There is no might nor power except with Allaah

اللهم إني أعوذ بك من البخل، وأعوذبك من الجبن، وأعوذ بك من أن ارد إلى أرذل العمر، وأعوذ بك من فتنة الدنيا وعذاب القبر

Oh Allah, I seek Your Protection from miserliness I seek Your Protection from cowardice, and I seek Your Protection from being returned to feeble old age. I seek Your Protection from the trials/troubles of this world and from the to rmentof the grave

بسم الله الذي لا يضر مع
اسمه شيء قي الأرض
ولا في السماء وهو
السميع العليم

"In the name of Allah
with whose Name
nothing is harmful on
Earth nor in the Heavens
and He is the All-
Hearing, the All-
Knowing.

"لا إله إلا الله وحده لا شريك له , له الملك و له الحمد و هو على كل شيء قدير"

"None has the right to be worshipped except Allah; He is One and has no partner. All the kingdom is for Him, and all the praises are for Him, and He is "Omnipotent"

يا حي يا قيوم برحمتك أستغيث اصلح لي شأني كله و لا تكلني إلى نفسي طرفة عين .

O Ever Living, O self-Subsisting and supporter of all, by Your Mercy I seek help, rectify for me all of my affairs and do not leave me depend on myself, even for the blink of an eye

اللهم إني أعوذ بك من البخل، وأعوذ بك من الجبن، وأعوذ بك من أن ارد إلى أرذل العمر، وأعوذ بك من فتنة الدنيا وعذاب القبر .

Oh Allah, I seek Your Protection from miserliness I seek Your Protection from cowardice, and I seek Your Protection from being returned to feeble old age. I seek Your Protection from the trials/troubles of this world and from the to rmentof the grave

اللهم انت ربي لا إله إلا أنت , خلقتني وأنا عبدك وأنا على عهدك ووعدك ما استطعت , أعوذبك من شر ما صنعت , أبوء لك بنعمتك علي وأبوء بذنبي فاغفر لي فإنه لا يغفر الذنوب إلا أنت

Oh Allah!, You are my Lord, there is No deitybut You. You Created me and I am Yourservant and I am trying my best to keepmy Oath (offaith) to You and to seekto live in the hope of Your Promise.I seek Refuge in You from my greatest evildeeds. I acknowledge Your Blessings uponme and my sins. So forgive me, for none but You can forgive sins

بسم الله الذي لا يضر مع
اسمه شيء في الأرض ولا
في السماء وهو السميع
العليم

"In the name of Allah
with whose Name
nothing is harmful on
Earth nor in the
Heavens and He is the
All-Hearing, the All-
Knowing."

أعوذ بكلمات الله التامات
من شر ما خلق

"I seek refuge in the perfect words of Allah from the Evil of what He has created".

اللهم عالم الغيب والشهادة فاطر السماوات و الأرض رب كل شيءٍ و مليكه , أشهد أن لا إله إلا أنت أعوذ بك من شر نفسي و من شر الشيطان و شركه , وان أقترف على نفسي سوءاً أو أجره إلى مسلم

Allah, Knower of the unseen and the seen, Creator of the Heavens and the Earth, Lord and sovereign of all things, I bear witness that none has the right to be worshipped except You. I seek in You from the evil of myself and from the evil of Shytan and his call to ShirkPolytheism), and from committing wrong against myself or bringing such upon another Muslim".

بسم الله ولجنا , وبسم الله خرجنا وعلى ربنا توكلنا

In the Name of Allah we enter , and in the Name of Allah we leave , and we trust in Our Lord

رَبَّنَا آتِنَا فِي الدُّنْيَا حَسَنَةً وَفِي الآخِرَةِ حَسَنَةً وَقِنَا عَذَابَ النَّارِ

Our Lord! Give us in this world that which is good and in the Hereafter that which is good, and save us from the torment of the Fire!

رَبَّنَا أَفْرِغْ عَلَيْنَا صَبْرًا وَثَبِّتْ أَقْدَامَنَا وَانصُرْنَا عَلَى الْقَوْمِ الْكَافِرِينَ

Our Lord! Pour forth on us patience and make us victorious over the disbelieving people.

رَبَّنَا لاَ تُزِغْ قُلُوبَنَا بَعْدَ إِذْ هَدَيْتَنَا وَهَبْ لَنَا مِن لَّدُنكَ رَحْمَةً إِنَّكَ أَنتَ الْوَهَّابُ

Our Lord! Let not our hearts deviate (from the truth) after You have guided us, and grant us mercy from You. Truly, You are the Bestower

رَبَّنَا إِنَّنَا آمَنَّا فَاغْفِرْ لَنَا ذُنُوبَنَا وَقِنَا عَذَابَ النَّارِ

Our Lord! We have indeed believed, so forgive us our sins and save us from the punishment of the Fire

رَبِّ هَبْ لِي مِن لَّدُنْكَ
ذُرِّيَّةً طَيِّبَةً إِنَّكَ سَمِيعُ
الدُّعَاءِ

O my Lord! Grant me from You, a good offspring. You are indeed the All-Hearer of invocation

رَّبَّنَا اغْفِرْ لَنَا ذُنُوبَنَا وَإِسْرَافَنَا فِي أَمْرِنَا وَثَبِّتْ أَقْدَامَنَا وانصُرْنَا عَلَى الْقَوْمِ الْكَافِرِينَ

Our Lord! Forgive us our sins and our transgressions (in keeping our duties to You), establish our feet firmly, and give us victory over the disbelieving folk

رَبَّنَا ظَلَمْنَا أَنفُسَنَا وَإِن لَّمْ تَغْفِرْ لَنَا وَتَرْحَمْنَا لَنَكُونَنَّ مِنَ الْخَاسِرِينَ

Our Lord! We have wronged ourselves. If You forgive us not, and bestow not upon us Your Mercy, we shall certainly be of the losers

رَبَّنَا لاَ تَجْعَلْنَا مَعَ الْقَوْمِ الظَّالِمِينَ

Our Lord! Place us not with the people who are Zaalimoon (polytheists and wrong doers

رَبِّ اجْعَلْنِي مُقِيمَ الصَّلَاةِ وَمِن ذُرِّيَّتِي رَبَّنَا وَتَقَبَّلْ دُعَاء

O my Lord! Make me one who performs As-Salaat (Iqaamat-as-Salaat), and (also) from my offspring, our Lord! And accept my invocation

آمين

amen

www.ingramcontent.com/pod-product-compliance
Lightning Source LLC
Chambersburg PA
CBHW051944150726
47999CB00006B/2355